To Hannah
with Love

From:
Grandma and Papa

LEAVE ONLY RIPPLES

A Canoe Country Sketchbook

Consie Powell

Raven Productions, Inc.   Ely, Minnesota

Library of Congress Cataloging-in-Publication Data

Powell, Consie.
  Leave only ripples : a canoe country sketchbook / Consie Powell.
    p. cm.
  Summary: "Describes a family canoe trip in the Quetico-Superior wilderness along the border between
Minnesota and Canada, including natural history and evidence of the fur trade era, Indian inhabitants, and
logging. Woodcuts and sketchbook entries illustrate the story"—Provided by publisher.
  ISBN 0-9677057-9-7 (hardcover : alk. paper)
  1. Canoes and canoeing—Quetico-Superior Country (Ont. and Minn.)—Pictorial works. 2. Quetico-Superior
Country (Ont. and Minn.)—Description and travel—Pictorial works. I. Title.
  GV776.15.O57P69 2005
  797.122'0977676—dc22
                    2005003575

Text and illustrations copyright © 2005 by Constance Buffington Powell
Published 2005 by Raven Productions, Inc. PO Box 188, Ely, MN 55731
        218.365.3375   www.ravenwords.com

For Rog,
my favorite stern—mate,
and Virginia,
my favorite bow—mate.

The illustrations were created with
hand—colored woodblock prints,
ink and watercolor drawings, and
field sketches drawn in the
Boundary Waters Canoe Area Wilderness
and Quetico Provincial Park.

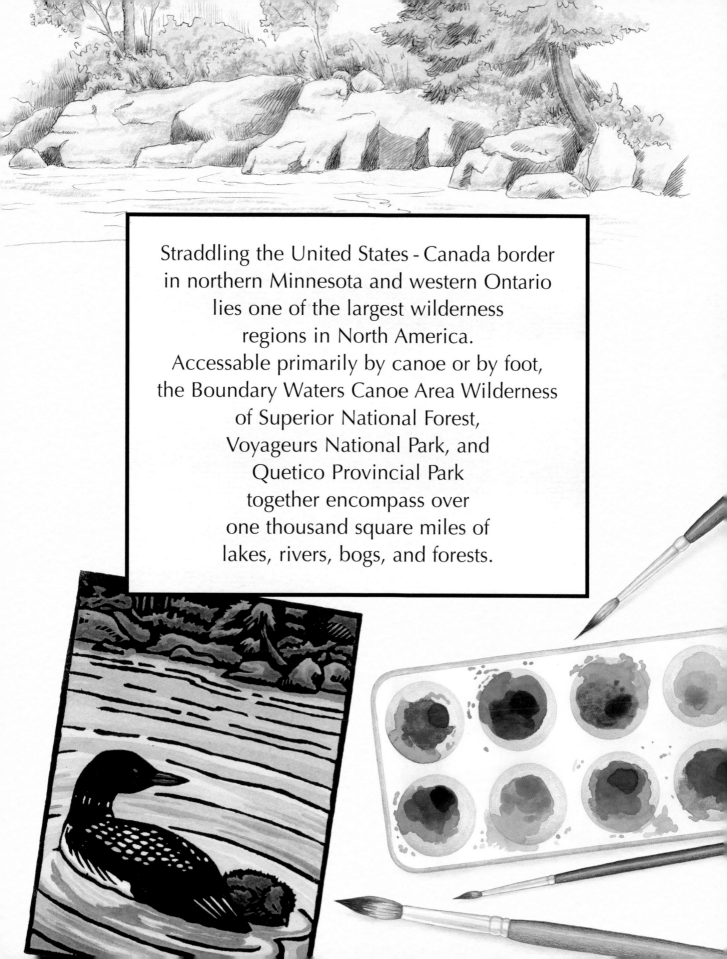

Straddling the United States - Canada border
in northern Minnesota and western Ontario
lies one of the largest wilderness
regions in North America.
Accessable primarily by canoe or by foot,
the Boundary Waters Canoe Area Wilderness
of Superior National Forest,
Voyageurs National Park, and
Quetico Provincial Park
together encompass over
one thousand square miles of
lakes, rivers, bogs, and forests.

clubmoss

fragrant
water lily

wild
columbine

fragrant
water lily
buds

bunchberry

Dawn comes early in July — the sun rises
while we still sleep. Like crayons in a box,
the three of us lie in brightly colored
sleeping bags, snug in our little tent.
In a few minutes
we will get up,
take a quick dip
in the lake,
and start
our day.

People have been
traveling through
this wild country for
a long time —
sometimes alone,
sometimes in groups. This time
we travel as a family.
Virginia paddles in the bow
and notices things the rest
of us miss. Roger paddles in
the stern, charts our course, and
shares nuggets of natural history.
Sketchbook in hand, I wield a pen
rather than a paddle, noting the
magic and beauty of plants and
animals, sounds and sights,
thoughts and ideas.

By words and sketches
we remember. We once
again hear a winter wren,
smell the balsam fir,
taste that big
sweet raspberry.
My sketchbook lets us
return to the
Canoe Country
whenever we wish.

birch
leaves
and
seeds

cedar

wild sarsaparilla

wild
lily-of-the-valley

*T*haap...Thaap... Thaap-thaap-thaap-thaap-thaap! Before you even open your eyes you hear webbed feet run across the water. Then, *"Woohoohoo-woohoohoo-woohoohoo!"* The loon is airborne and yodels as she flies off to another lake. Cozy and warm, you lie in your sleeping bag as you listen to the sounds of early morning. *Chunk-ker-splash!* A leopard frog hits the water. *Bop-bop-bop-bop-bop!* A pileated woodpecker searches for breakfast. *"Chr-r-r-r-r-r!"* A red squirrel scolds you for pitching your tent under his favorite white pine.

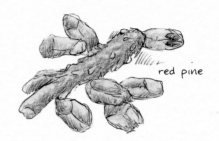

red pine

A naked core and cone scales littering the ground show us where a red squirrel feasted.

Starting at the stem end, the squirrel peels the scales away from the cone to get the seeds.

white pine

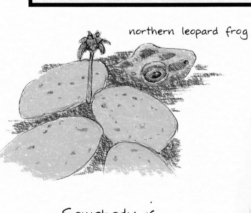

northern leopard frog

Somebody is hiding among the water shield leaves.

Our morning view out the tent

The loon finally takes flight.

When we find
great chunks of bark
on the ground we look up to
find where a pileated woodpecker
has been working.

Blueberry pancakes — yum! And the leftover berries for a breakfast dessert.

We have stuff sacks for everything — meals, dishes, sleeping bags, tent.

An eight—legged friend has taken shelter in the pack overnight — Virginia fishes it out...

Into the Duluth pack they go...

and somehow, we make everything fit.

Tuck away the breakfast dishes, take down the tent, and stow your gear once again in sturdy canvas packs. You can smell the misty freshness of a new day — another day to explore sparkling lakes and towering forests, to paddle winding creeks and open waters, to hike across portage trails laced with feathermoss and wintergreen. Each day your canoe carries you deeper into this wild land .

Our dishes dry for a few minutes before we pack them away.

A broken wintergreen leaf has such a wonderful minty aroma, and tastes good too. Better than chewing gum!

We douse the fire with water and stir the ashes until they are cold to touch. We leave a little kindling and some birchbark for the next camper to start a fire.

Can you imagine when this broad slab of granite beneath your feet was a mountain? Long, long ago, before humans or other animals lived on earth, molten rock cooled, buckled and thrusted upward to form the great Laurentian mountain range. The weather of eons leveled and scoured it. Now, billions of years later, you walk on ancient bedrock slabs of gabbro and greenstone.

Colors are brighter when the rocks are wet.

The rocks and pebbles are shades of pink and green and grey.

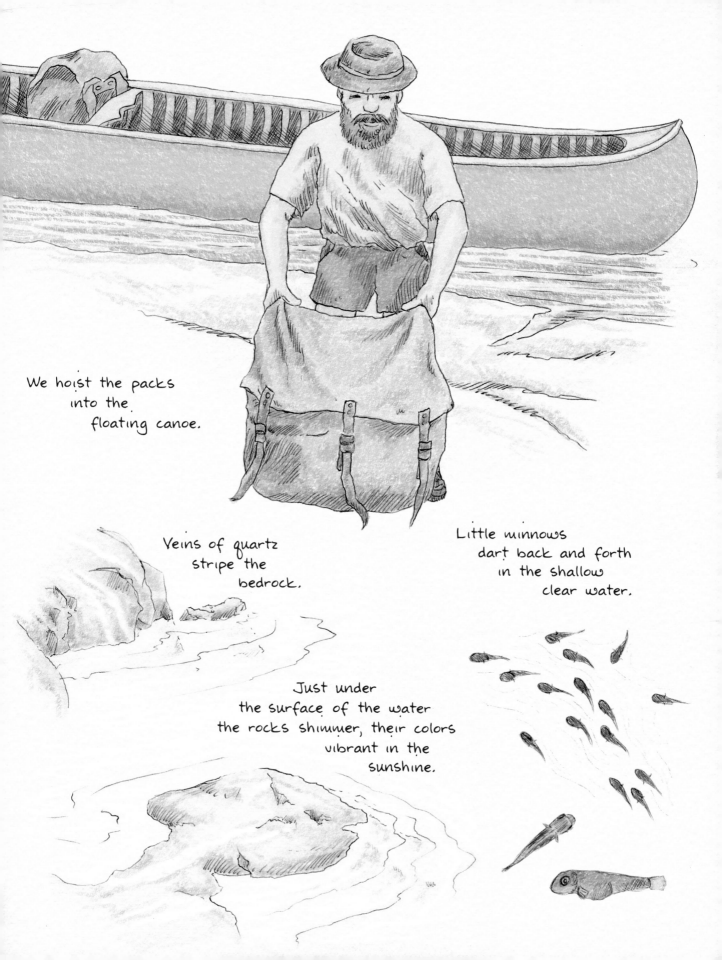

We hoist the packs
into the
floating canoe.

Veins of quartz
stripe the
bedrock.

Little minnows
dart back and forth
in the shallow
clear water.

Just under
the surface of the water
the rocks shimmer, their colors
vibrant in the
sunshine.

As you paddle, you skirt stone reefs and pass high rock bluffs. Thousands of years ago, huge blankets of ice covered the land with crushing weight and unrelenting cold. As the glaciers moved, they scraped and gouged, carving out these lakes. Imagine icy glaciers leaving these giant boulders like a pile of monstrous marbles.

A painted turtle basks in the warm morning sun. We stop paddling and glide by quietly, so he stays put.

Above the high water marks we see rock tripe lichens...

and a fishing spider.

Rock polypody ferns grow from tiny cracks.

Stripes of pollen on the shoreline rocks show the higher water levels of last spring.

Pink corydalis grows on these open rocky outcrops.

It looks delicate, but it is a tough little flower.

An osprey flies overhead — we know him by his bent wings in flight.

The packs are heavy, but the flowers are wonderful.

pink ladyslipper

blue—bead lily

Virginia finds an old vireo nest.

In the cool woods we notice shelf fungi...

and other lovely mushrooms.

Roger disappears up the portage
with his pack and the canoe.
We move a bit more slowly — and
find some treasures that show
us who else was here...

scat on a rock —
probably a
weasel

A mama grouse
tries to draw
our attention
away from
her chicks.
It almost
works,
until
Virginia
spies   3 little
          fuzzballs...

Sapsucker holes in a
birch tree

We watch a
red squirrel
lick the
drips of sap —
guess who
has a
sweet tooth!?

Hundreds of narrow portage trails connect these lakes. They wind past orchid-studded bogs, through shadowy forests, around rushing rapids. The trails are old, created by early Natives and later traveled by explorers and traders. Wild animals use them, too. Bent beneath your pack, look carefully as you cross the portage. Here are stones worn smooth of lichens by many generations of moccasins and boots. And there, in the soft mud, is the fresh print of a wolf. Was it her howl you heard beneath the stars last night?

A mother merganser
and her huge brood —
we count 16 ducklings!

Wild rice
flowers
in the
shallows.

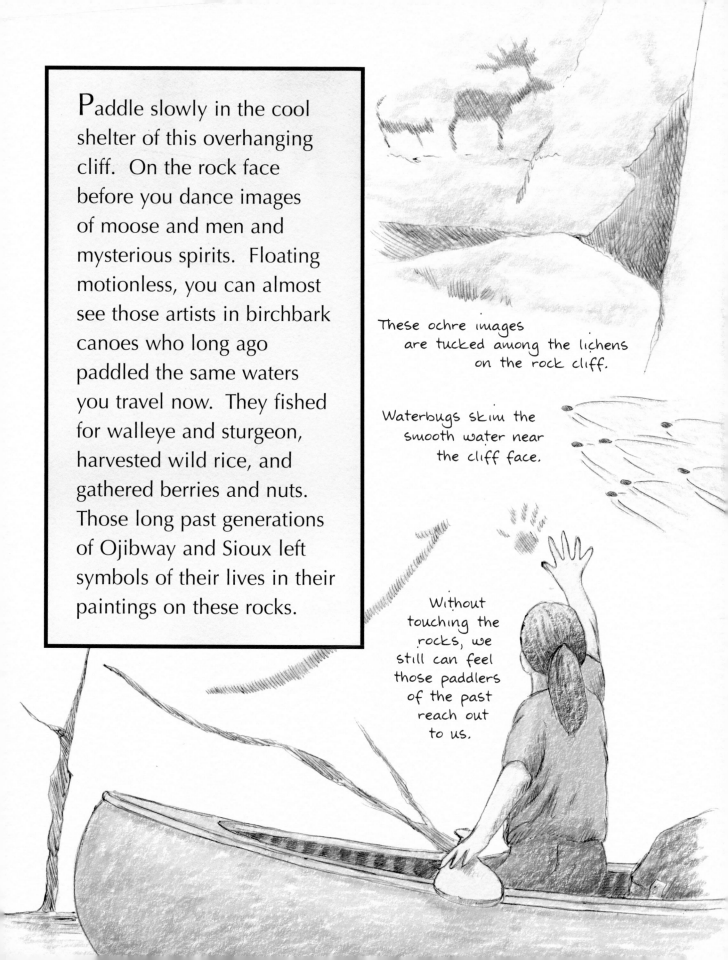

Paddle slowly in the cool shelter of this overhanging cliff. On the rock face before you dance images of moose and men and mysterious spirits. Floating motionless, you can almost see those artists in birchbark canoes who long ago paddled the same waters you travel now. They fished for walleye and sturgeon, harvested wild rice, and gathered berries and nuts. Those long past generations of Ojibway and Sioux left symbols of their lives in their paintings on these rocks.

These ochre images are tucked among the lichens on the rock cliff.

Waterbugs skim the smooth water near the cliff face.

Without touching the rocks, we still can feel those paddlers of the past reach out to us.

On a narrow point ahead a lofty white pine towers above the spruce and cedars. It is thick and bristly at the top, but cut bare of branches in the middle. This is a lob tree, shaped by Voyageurs during an era of commerce between Native beaver trappers and French traders. Two centuries ago it first marked the Voyageurs' route. How many canoes have passed this old lob tree since a sharp axe shaped it?

Alder leaves and the tiny, exquisite cones

The big white pine is old and scraggly — but its silhouette stands bold against the sky.

Cedars lean out over the water to reach for light. Their flat bottoms show us where deer reached up from the frozen lake to browse during winter.

That swimming shape is a beaver — no one else would carry a branch.

Fresh, floating beaver sticks are bright yellow or white — older ones look grayish.

big teeth marks

Virginia retrieves a piece to carve later.

A big green darner dragonfly lands on the bow of our canoe.

red pine

pine
seedlings

white pine

round cone
2 stout needles

long cone
5 delicate needles

A herring gull leaves its perch on a deadhead.

A pair of black terns dive—bombs us again and again. Do they have a nest nearby?

The bay leading to our next portage is full of old water—logged timber.

Guide your canoe carefully past that floating deadhead log. It is a waterlogged remnant of a huge logjam, left from the logging boom a hundred years ago, when great expanses of untouched forest were cut and stripped of giant pine trees. You see other reminders of the long-gone lumberjacks: here a bay full of deadheads, there a rusted mooring ring that once anchored rafts of logs. All around you is a thick, green forest — but the giant trees are gone. Will young pines grow old enough to become as majestic as their ancestors once were?

As we paddle through the narrows, we spy a huge iron mooring ring anchored into the lakeside granite.

The Joe—Pye weed growing in the clearing is covered with Aphrodite butterflies.

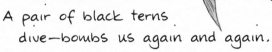

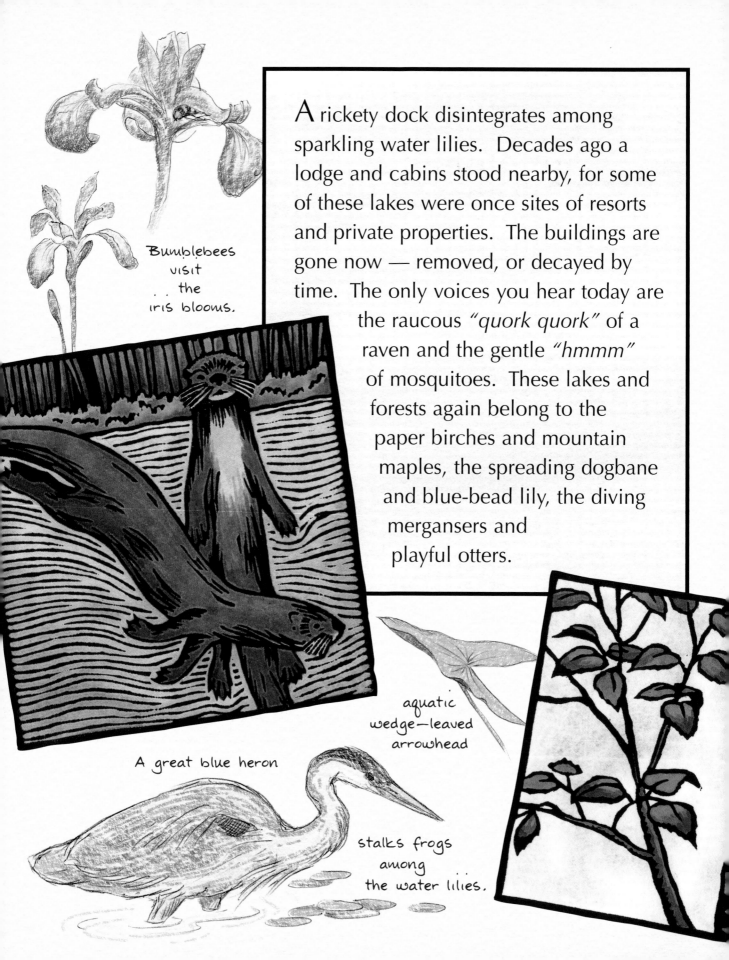

Bumblebees
visit
. . the
iris blooms.

A rickety dock disintegrates among sparkling water lilies. Decades ago a lodge and cabins stood nearby, for some of these lakes were once sites of resorts and private properties. The buildings are gone now — removed, or decayed by time. The only voices you hear today are the raucous *"quork quork"* of a raven and the gentle *"hmmm"* of mosquitoes. These lakes and forests again belong to the paper birches and mountain maples, the spreading dogbane and blue-bead lily, the diving mergansers and playful otters.

aquatic
wedge—leaved
arrowhead

A great blue heron

stalks frogs
among
. . the water lilies.

A snapping turtle swims in the shallows.

Mountain maple still holds its winged seeds.

Over the water hang fruits some folks call juneberries or serviceberries. We call them saskatoons, and find them delicious!

A green frog holds very still...

A few rotting boards stick out from the sweet gale bushes.

Uphill from tonight's campsite, scorched and tumbled trees mix with lush new growth. Within the velvet black debris stands the skeleton of a tall red pine killed by the lightning bolt that started a fire here last summer. Hidden inside the trunk, hungry beetle grubs buzz as they gnaw the dead wood. Charred branches rot and crumble — their nutrients returned to the earth by rain and snow. Warmed by bright sunshine, jack pine seedlings, brilliant fireweed, and dense blueberry shrubs thrive in this fresh rich soil. From the ashes of a burned forest sprout the seedlings of a new infant forest.

Unloading the canoe at the end of the day

Fireweed grows on the hillside.

jack pine seedling

2 or 3 needles — coarse and a bit twisty

cones

closed tightly

opened by the heat of a fire

Blueberries are growing
everywhere, and
the bushes are loaded.
We shall feast!

A weathered old deer
antler shows
mouse tooth marks.
Better than
a vitamin pill,
a few chomps on
an antler give
a rodent a healthy
dose of calcium.

A big old scat is
full of pits and seeds
and even whole berries —
the bears are
eating well
this summer.

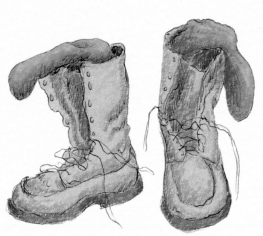

A cluster of chokecherries glows red as the afternoon sun shines through the fruit.

Boots and socks sit in the warm sun to dry.

British soldiers and pixie cup lichens are everywhere.

Soft feathermoss carpets the edges of our campsite.

A kingfisher rattles past over the open water.

Beach your canoe now, unload the packs and set your paddle to rest. From deep in the cool forest you hear the mellow flute of a hermit thrush. In the shallows across the lake you notice a moose dining on water lily roots. A gentle breeze brushes your cheeks and peaceful quiet surrounds you. You have become part of the wilderness.

We share this campsite with a tolerant big toad...

Chickadees come to investigate as we set up camp.

Red—winged blackbirds call from the cattails in a quiet little bay.

and 3 curious grey jays.

Virginia whittles her beaver stick while we fix supper.

Softly, night wraps a cloak of darkness around you. Overhead, the aurora borealis twists and dances in an indigo silence. You relax now, feeling the sweet fatigue that comes from the miles you paddled and hiked today. Your mind is at peace.

Our tent is nestled between boulders, a pin cherry bush, and several young aspens.

Large-leaved aster growing around the edges of our camp is just starting to send up flower buds.

A pot of stew simmers on the fire.

A tiger moth flutters into camp —
  lights upon our packs
    for a moment — then is gone.

The
beaverwood
  carving
    takes shape.

As
  dark
    falls

we watch a
  deer mouse
    peek out,

      then
        tiptoe
      over

and
  snoop in
an empty
cocoa cup.

Tomorrow you will paddle to new lakes and discover new wonders. You will float on waters that carried birchbark canoes and walk along trails in the footsteps of the Voyageurs.

In the bog,
 pitcher plants hide
  and cotton grass
   nods in
    the wind...

and tucked almost
 out of sight,
  but not quite —
 glistening sundews
   and tiny
  rose pogonia
   orchids.

The blue jay feather is dwarfed by an eagle feather.

A tree frog takes shelter in our canoe for the night...

But as you pass through this land of solitude and sunsets, you will leave no sign at all. You take memories in your heart, images in your journal, and behind, you leave only ripples.

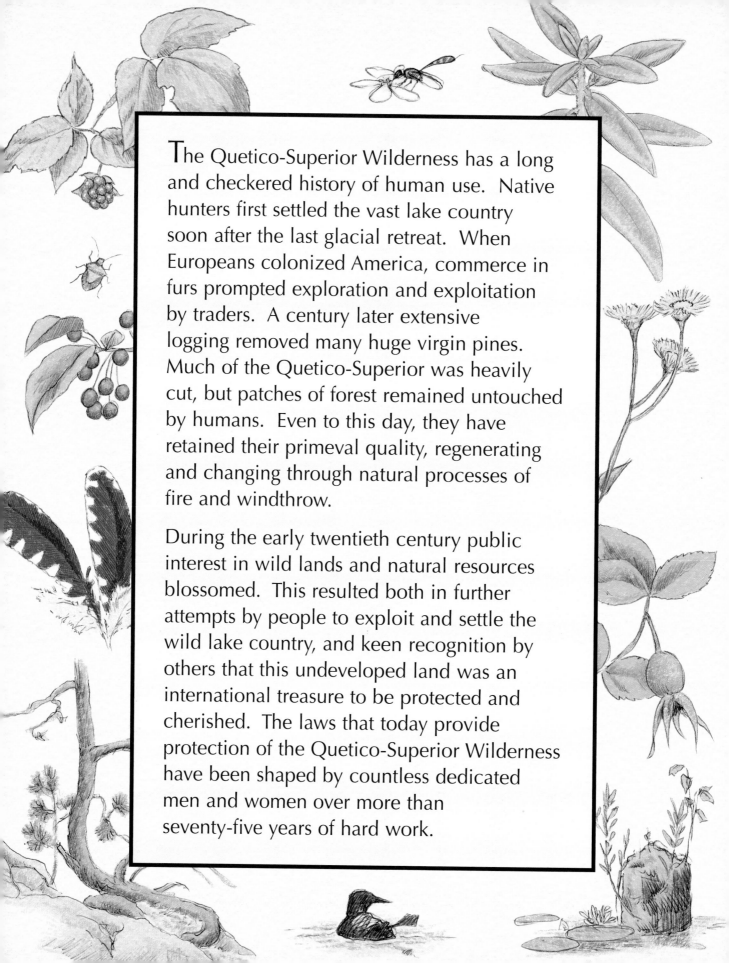

The Quetico-Superior Wilderness has a long and checkered history of human use. Native hunters first settled the vast lake country soon after the last glacial retreat. When Europeans colonized America, commerce in furs prompted exploration and exploitation by traders. A century later extensive logging removed many huge virgin pines. Much of the Quetico-Superior was heavily cut, but patches of forest remained untouched by humans. Even to this day, they have retained their primeval quality, regenerating and changing through natural processes of fire and windthrow.

During the early twentieth century public interest in wild lands and natural resources blossomed. This resulted both in further attempts by people to exploit and settle the wild lake country, and keen recognition by others that this undeveloped land was an international treasure to be protected and cherished. The laws that today provide protection of the Quetico-Superior Wilderness have been shaped by countless dedicated men and women over more than seventy-five years of hard work.